SUPER DC HEROES

BATMAN

SCARECROW, DOCTOR OF FEAR

WRITTEN BY
MATTHEW K. MANNING

ILLUSTRATED BY
ERIK DOESCHER,
MIKE DeCARLO, AND
LEE LOUGHRIDGE

BATMAN CREATED BY
BOB KANE

www.raintreepublishers.co.uk
Visit our website to find out
more information about
Raintree books.

To order:
☎ Phone 0845 6044371
🖷 Fax +44 (0) 1865 312263
✉ Email myorders@raintreepublishers.co.uk

Customers from outside the UK please telephone +44 1865 312262

Raintree is an imprint of Capstone Global Library Limited,
a company incorporated in England and Wales having its
registered office at 7 Pilgrim Street, London, EC4V 6LB
– Registered company number: 6695582

First published by Stone Arch Books in 2011
First published in hardback and paperback in the
United Kingdom by Capstone Global Library in 2011
The moral rights of the proprietor have been asserted.

Art Director: Bob Lentz
Designer: Brann Garvey
Production Specialist: Michelle Biedscheid
Editor: Vaarunika Dharmapala
Originated by Capstone Global Library Ltd
Printed and bound in China by Leo Paper Products Ltd

ISBN 978 1 406 22536 5 (hardback)
15 14 13 12 11
10 9 8 7 6 5 4 3 2 1

ISBN 978 1 406 22541 9 (paperback)
15 14 13 12 11
10 9 8 7 6 5 4 3 2 1

British Library Cataloguing in Publication Data
A full catalogue record for this book is available
from the British Library.

CONTENTS

CHAPTER 1

THE FIRE DRILL 4

CHAPTER 2

A THOROUGH EXAM 14

CHAPTER 3

A BRUSH WITH DEATH 20

CHAPTER 4

THE ROOT OF THE PROBLEM 31

CHAPTER 5

A NEW APPOINTMENT 38

POLICE FILE 50
BIOGRAPHIES 52
GLOSSARY 53
DISCUSSION QUESTIONS 54
WRITING PROMPTS 55

THE FIRE DRILL

Dan Reiner was having a long day. When his friend had Jill called in sick, Dan had offered to cover her shift at Berger's department store. He had been behind the till for nearly twelve hours and was ready to call it a night.

Dan glanced down at his watch. It was five minutes until ten o'clock – almost time to cash up.

"Ahem," came a voice from in front of him. Dan looked up to see an elderly woman with a scowl on her face.

"Sorry, madam," said Dan, "I didn't see you there."

"Yes, yes," replied the old woman. She pushed a grey jumper across the counter. "I want to pay and I don't have all night."

CLICK! Suddenly, all the lights in the department store went out. The elderly woman stopped talking. Everyone was alarmed. After all, Berger's was Gotham City's largest department store. It was hard enough to find your way round with the lights on.

"Hey!" a voice shouted from across the room. Dan strained his eyes to see through the darkness. He could barely make out the shadow of a man standing near the exit sign. "What's going on?" the man yelled. "The doors are locked!"

Dan stumbled towards the man, pushing through the crowd at the exit. He tried the door, but it would not budge. The man was right. Without the store manager's key, they would all be trapped for a while.

Dan looked at the panicked shoppers running around. He knew his long day was not over yet.

*   *   *

Minutes away, Batgirl was trying her best to keep up with Batman. **BANG!** Shooting her grapnel gun into the night air, the young super hero could see her mentor two buildings ahead. She rolled her eyes. She was sure he was going faster just to annoy her.

The super-strong cable from Batgirl's grapnel gun caught hold. It wrapped around a gargoyle's head on a nearby roof.

With a running start, she jumped off the rooftop. Then she swung round the building's side. Using her gymnastics training, she flipped herself on to the ledge of the following building. **THUD!** There, across the roof, stood Batman. His cape blew gently in the breeze. **FLAP! FLAP!**

"What's the matter?" Batgirl asked the Dark Knight. "Getting a little tired in your old age?"

Batman pointed to the street below. "Down there," he said. Then he jumped off the rooftop.

Batgirl watched him swing down to one of the entrances of Berger's department store. At first, she did not notice anything out of the ordinary. It looked like a normal crowd of people standing by the store's doors. Then suddenly…

Batgirl's eyes widened. Someone had thrown a mannequin through one of the doors' glass panels. Dozens of people shoved their way out of the small opening. Someone was going to get hurt.

On the ground, Batman knelt in front of the doors. **CLINK CLINK** He picked the lock with a tool from his Utility Belt. When Batgirl landed beside him, he had already finished. He swung the double doors wide open. The panicked crowd burst out of the entrance and on to the pavement.

Batman looked over at Batgirl. "You take care of the other exits," he said. He started pushing his way through the crowd.

"Where are you going?" Batgirl called after him.

"To find out who did this," he said.

As Batgirl helped a woman to her feet, she tried to see where Batman had gone. He had already disappeared into the silent shadows.

Meanwhile, Batman ran up the stalled escalator to the top floor. He sprinted past the perfume aisle to the employee break room at the back of the store.

Batman already had a good idea of who he was hunting. After all, the tills had not been touched. There did not seem to be any stolen merchandise. The criminal who shut off the lights and locked the doors had done it purely to cause chaos. Batman knew of only one man who lived purely to frighten others. His name was Jonathan Crane, the fear-obsessed criminal also known as the Scarecrow.

CLINK CLINK Batman easily picked the lock on the employee break room door. He slowly pushed it open. Down a long, dark corridor, a shadow slipped through a doorway. Batman raced after him.

Turning a corner, Batman peered into a maintenance room. Moonlight trickled into the room from above, lighting a ladder that led up to an open rooftop hatch. Without hesitating, the Dark Knight climbed to the rooftop. He surveyed the scene.

A lone figure stood in the shadows at the base of the building's water tower. "Why did you have to spoil my fun, Batman?" asked the figure.

"Someone could have been hurt, Crane," Batman said, slowly walking towards him. With his right hand, Batman reached into the back of his Utility Belt.

"Who's a crane?" said the man in the shadows. "I'm not a crane."

"Move into the light," Batman said, ignoring his foe's crazy ramblings. "Slowly." As he spoke, Batman secretly removed a Batarang from his belt.

"But that ruins the mystery," said the man. "And there's no fear without an element of the unknown."

ZING! Batman hurled the Batarang across the rooftop. Its thick cord trailed behind it in the air. The Batarang wrapped around the darkened figure. **THUD!** The man fell over into the moonlight.

The man in front of Batman was not Scarecrow. He certainly was not Jonathan Crane. In fact, Batman had never seen this man before in his life.

CHAPTER 2

A THOROUGH EXAM

"Are you still at it?" Batgirl asked. She was walking down the stairs to the Batcave.

"Hmm," Batman answered. He continued to stare at the screen of the Batcomputer in front of him.

"You know, that's not really a response," Batgirl said.

"Sorry," Batman said. "I was lost in thought."

"Any leads?" Batgirl asked. She was looking up at the large computer monitor.

"None to speak of," Batman said. "His name is David Scheeve. He's just an ordinary store manager. No criminal record. No mental health issues. He's worked at Berger's department store for more than twelve years."

"Doesn't sound like your typical Arkham Asylum patient," Batgirl said. She studied Scheeve's image on the computer screen. "Any connection with Professor Crane?"

"None that I can find," Batman said. He opened another window on his screen and began typing notes. "All his personal contacts check out. Most people seem to think he's nice, well-meaning, and quiet."

"Are you sure we're talking about the same man here?" Batgirl asked. "Last night, he wouldn't shut up even after you handcuffed him."

"It's completely out of character for this man," Batman said. He stood up, shrugged his shoulders, and yawned. "What time is it anyway, Barbara?"

"It's almost seven thirty in the morning," Batgirl said. "You've been down here on the computer all night."

Batman turned and walked into the shadows of the Batcave. "I need you to call Wayne Enterprises and apologize for me," he said to Batgirl.

"Apologize?" Batgirl asked. "For what?" She heard Batman's boots stepping softly in the darkness, the click of a cabinet door, and the rustle of his cape. **FLAP! FLAP!**

"I was supposed to be at an early meeting with the board members," Batman said from the shadows.

"Looks like I might be late," added the Dark Knight.

"Do you have an excuse in mind for the board members?" Batgirl asked.

"Tell them I was out shopping," Batman replied.

"Yeah, like they'll believe that," Batgirl said. She started laughing to herself. "You have twenty versions of the same black suit. What on Earth could you possibly be shopping for?"

Bruce Wayne, Batman's secret alter ego, stepped out of the shadows. He was dressed in one of his signature business suits and carrying a briefcase.

"How about a new crime-fighting partner?" he said, giving Batgirl a teasing smirk.

As he headed up the stairs to Wayne Manor, Batgirl called after him. "Okay," she said. "But you're going to have to break the news to Robin."

"Enough jokes," Bruce said, exiting the room. "Just make the call."

CHAPTER 3

A BRUSH WITH DEATH

The lift in Wayne Tower was much slower than normal. Bruce looked down at his watch. It was nearly eight. The board would be furious, if they were even still waiting for him. *Oh well,* Bruce thought. It was good cover. The more people who thought Bruce Wayne was a lazy billionaire, the fewer who would connect him to Batman.

Bruce looked around the crowded lift. No one was saying anything. They were in his building, after all.

Most of the employees at Wayne Enterprises knew their boss when they saw him. It made sense that they would be on their best behaviour. After all, they rarely had an opportunity to share a lift with him. Bruce smiled politely at the man standing beside him. The man tried not to look nervous as he smiled back. Around his office, Bruce Wayne had the same impact that Batman had in a room full of criminals.

SKREEEEEEECH!

Suddenly, the lift ground to a halt. Bruce regained his balance. He looked around the lift. His employees all appeared a bit concerned, if not outright terrified. And then, just as suddenly – **SNAP!** The lift began to drop. The cables had been cut.

Many of Bruce's fellow passengers began screaming. Bruce looked up at the ceiling. All the lifts in his buildings came equipped with escape hatches for this sort of emergency.

Just as he was about to act, the lift stopped. Several passengers were knocked to the floor. Others steadied themselves by clutching the walls. Bruce remained upright among them. He held tight to his briefcase with one hand. With his other, he helped the man next to him stay on his feet. The man looked at Bruce and attempted another nervous smile.

"Th-thank you, s-s-sir," the man said, just as the lift began rising again. It was moving at a speed much faster than normal. **ZZRRRRTT!** The lights inside the lift began flickering on and off.

Many of the passengers were screaming again. Some had their eyes shut, waiting for this horrible nightmare to be over. Then the lift began to plummet again.

The lift continued to fall and its lights continued to switch on and off. If the man Bruce had helped was not frightened before, he certainly was now. The man looked over at Bruce, but Mr Wayne was nowhere to be seen! Somehow, he had disappeared into thin air. The man began to scream as the lift stopped suddenly once again.

If the man had glanced upwards, he would have seen his billionaire boss disappearing through the escape hatch. Bruce Wayne had used the flickering light to his advantage.

During a moment of darkness, he had made his escape. Bruce closed the hatch behind him and looked up the lift shaft. There was no one around. He quickly pulled open his shirt, revealing the black bat-symbol underneath. He was glad he had kept his work clothes on. He had had a feeling he would need them today.

Bruce quickly shed the rest of his business suit. He snapped open the latches on his briefcase and gathered his mask, cape, boots, and gloves from inside. In moments, Bruce Wayne was no longer standing there. In his place stood Batman.

Then the lift began to drop again! Batman leapt up into the air. As gravity took hold of him, he pulled his grapnel gun out of his belt and fired it upwards. POP!

CHING! The grapnel's hook stuck to the top of the shaft near the lift cables. Batman pushed a button on the device, and the grapnel lifted him up.

Batman looked up at the top of the shaft. It was getting closer every second. Just then, the Dark Knight noticed that the doors to the top floor seemed to be open. As he soared up towards them, Batman spotted the shadow of a man standing in the doorway.

But Batman's first worry was the lift falling below him. The Dark Knight pulled a small capsule from his belt. He threw the pellet above him at the two giant pulleys that controlled the cables. **KRAK!** The capsule shattered. Ice crystals instantly poured out of it and formed around the pulleys and the thick cables.

Within seconds, the machinery ground to a halt. The cables were frozen solid, and the lift was stuck in place. The passengers were safe – at least for now.

Batman reached the open doorway and swung himself into the lobby of the sixtieth floor. He quickly got to his feet and looked up at the stunned receptionist sitting behind her desk across the room. She was too shocked to speak. Instead, she pointed a shaky finger at the emergency exit on her left. Batman nodded and raced into the stairwell.

A man in an orange vest ran down the stairs. He had a head start and was already two stories below Batman. Even from that distance, Batman could see that the man's hands were covered in grease. He had to be the one who had sabotaged the lift.

As he chased after the man, Batman pulled a few round pellets out of his belt. He hurled them down the stairs in front of him. *Hisssssss* Smoke began to leak out of the capsules as they hit the steps. Batman pulled a small breathing device from his belt and put it between his teeth. He continued on into the fog.

A few stories more and he caught up to his prey. The man in the vest was lying on the fifty-fourth floor, gasping for breath through the thick smoke. Batman studied the man's features. But just like the manager from Berger's department store, he did not recognize him at all.

"You … ruined everything," the man said, gasping for air. "There was so much fear. They were so very afraid."

"Who sent you?" Batman growled.

"Who sent *you*?" the man muttered, dropping his head to the floor. Batman's knockout gas had worked too well. The man was out cold. As the smoke began to clear in the stairwell, Batman still felt lost in a fog.

CHAPTER 4

THE ROOT OF THE PROBLEM

The door to Gary Cosh's office creaked as it opened slowly. A figure entered the room. He did not bother turning on the light. After all, Batman works best in the dark.

Batman switched on a torch from his Utility Belt. **CLICK!** He held it between his teeth, sat in front of a big cabinet, and browsed through the files. The Dark Knight leafed through old phone records, expense reports, and employee reviews. He was searching for anything that could shed some light on these confusing crimes.

Batman moved over to the nearby desk in the small room. He took the torch out of his mouth and pressed the side of his cowl. **BZZT!**

"What's up, boss?" Batgirl's voice asked in his ear.

"I need you to take a look at something," Batman said into his communicator. "Do you still have David Scheeve's file open on the Batcomputer?"

"One sec," Batgirl said over radio. "Okay, here it is. What do you need to know, Bruce?"

"I'm in the office of one of the maintenance workers here at Wayne Enterprises," Batman said. "His name is Gary Cosh. Any connection to David Scheeve or Jonathan Crane?"

Back in the Batcave, Batgirl ran a search through the Batcomputer files. It displayed zero results. "Nothing," she said into the microphone on the Batcomputer's dashboard. "I don't see anything in Scheeve's file about a Gary Cosh."

"Hmph," Batman grunted. He began to flick through a diary on the maintenance worker's desk.

"Let me guess," Batgirl said. "You found another crazy guy."

"Just like before," Batman said. "This man was also obsessed with spreading fear and had no criminal record. He worked for my company for years without any incidents or complaints."

"So you're still thinking Scarecrow's behind this somehow?" Batgirl asked.

"My guess is that he's altered his fear gas," Batman said, turning the pages in the calendar in front of him.

"Instead of just making you panicked, this new gas creates the desire to cause panic in others?" questioned Batgirl. "Doesn't seem too efficient."

"What it seems like is another one of Jonathan Crane's sick experiments," Batman said.

Suddenly, Batman stopped flicking through the maintenance worker's diary. Yesterday's date was circled in red along with a crude drawing of a tooth. "Batgirl, did Scheeve have a dental appointment recently?" asked the Dark Knight.

"Hold on, let me hack into his health records," Batgirl said as she began typing.

"As a matter of fact, he did!" Batgirl exclaimed. "Two days ago, he had an appointment at Gentle Dental on Main Street," Batgirl said. "Is that helpful?"

Batgirl sat by the computer and waited for a response. It did not come. "Well," she said to herself. "I suppose that's a 'yes'."

CHAPTER 5

A NEW APPOINTMENT

Sonita Henry hated going to the dentist. In fact, just the faint sound of the drill coming from down the corridor was enough to make her squirm in her chair. She looked around the room. *It's so dark for a dentist's office*, she thought. Everything seemed old and dusty. Even the mirror next to her chair's water bowl was cracked.

"Are we ready?" came a voice behind her.

Sonita jumped in surprise. Her dentist had just entered the room.

Sonita could not really see his features under his surgical mask. All she could tell was that he had dark, lively eyes, and a skinny frame.

"Um, I suppose so," she said.

"We'll start with a little anaesthetic," said the dentist. He walked over to a small gas tank. It was attached to a short tube with a breathing mask on the end. "Wouldn't want you to feel anything unpleasant," he said as he carried the tank over to Sonita.

"What is that?" asked Sonita.

"It's just laughing gas," said the strange doctor. "We're called Gentle Dental for a reason." Sonita shrugged her shoulders and leant back. The dentist placed the breathing mask over her nose and mouth.

"Now just relax and breathe deeply," said the dentist. Sonita could not be sure, but it looked like he might be smiling beneath his own mask.

ZHHINNGG!

Sonita looked down at the thick tube connected to the breathing mask. It had been sliced in two by what looked like a sharp black ninja star. She looked closely at the small weapon now stuck deep into a wooden cabinet next to her. It was shaped like a bat.

She looked back at the dentist. He was staring wide-eyed at the doorway. Suddenly, he flew across the room. **THUD!** His frail body collided with the wall. Something had hit him. Sonita looked round. Behind her, almost blending in with the shadows themselves, was Batman.

"Hold your breath and run," Batman said to her. Sonita obeyed the crime fighter. She got up and sprinted for the exit.

Batman looked over at the severed tube, which was leaking a green gas. He covered his mouth.

Across the room, the dentist ripped his surgical mask off, revealing the face of the Scarecrow!

He looked more crazed than usual. Batman instantly realized the reason. Scarecrow was already obsessed with the idea of spreading fear. Now, he was inhaling his own new fear gas, increasing that obsession.

"I was always afraid of the dentist when I was a little kid," Scarecrow said. "It seemed like a fitting place to spread a little terror."

Batman did not respond. He moved slowly and cautiously towards his enemy.

"You know the thing about my new fear gas, Batman?" Scarecrow asked, reaching into the drawer of a nearby cabinet. "I couldn't work out all the side effects." The villain pulled a matchbook out of the drawer. "For instance," he said as he struck a match, "it's quite flammable!"

Batman raced towards Scarecrow, but it was too late. The villain flicked the lit match at the leaking gas tank.

Batman felt a ringing in his ears, and then his body struck the wall. He was lucky that the force of the explosion had not knocked him unconscious, or worse. Around him, the room was on fire – and Scarecrow was nowhere to be seen.

Batman got to his feet and raced into the corridor. He saw the villain running away, but there was nowhere to hide. The last room had no other exits. It was just a storage cupboard.

"Your experiments end here, Scarecrow," Batman said.

"That's what you think, Batman!" shouted the villain.

Scarecrow lunged at Batman with both hands. "Ahhh!" the villain screamed.

Batman stepped to the side like a matador dodging a mad bull. Then the Dark Knight spun and kicked Scarecrow in the back. **THWACK!** Scarecrow tumbled to the tile floor.

"Cough! Cough!" Scarecrow could barely find the strength to look up at his foe. He had breathed in too much gas and hit the ground too hard.

Batman lifted the villain up and placed handcuffs around his wrists. **CLINK CLINK** He could hear police sirens arriving outside the building. It looked like Batgirl had done a bit of work at her end as well.

Batman led the stumbling Scarecrow through the burning corridor to the building's front door. He shoved Scarecrow in the direction of the two police officers standing outside. Batman remained in the doorway. Thick, black smoke billowed out all round the super hero.

The officers helped Scarecrow to his feet. Before they could lead him to their patrol cars, Scarecrow looked back at his enemy.

Batman's voice growled out of the black cloud. "You're finished, Scarecrow," he said. "No one will be spreading fear in Gotham for a long time."

Scarecrow tossed his head back and laughed. "Oh, I hope you're joking," he said when he finally regained control of himself. "After all, Batman, who do you think gave me the idea in the first place?"

The police officers glanced over at the doorway to see Batman's reaction, but there was no one there. He had disappeared into the night, soaring above the darkened streets on his grapnel wire.

For once, Scarecrow was right. The evil-doers of Gotham City would continue to fear one thing – Batman, the World's Greatest Crime Fighter.

Scarecrow

REAL NAME: Professor Jonathan Crane

OCCUPATION: Professional criminal

BASE: Gotham City

HEIGHT:
1 m 83 cm

WEIGHT:
63 kg

EYES:
Blue

HAIR:
Brown

Jonathan Crane's obsession with fear took hold at an early age. Terrorized by bullies, Crane sought to free himself from his own worst fears. As he researched the subject of dread, Crane developed a strong understanding of fear. Using this knowledge, Crane overcame his tormentors by using their worst fears against them. This victory led to his transformation into the creepy super-villain, the Scarecrow.

G.C.P.D. GOTHAM CITY POLICE DEPARTMENT

- Crane became a professor at Gotham University to further his terrifying research. When his colleagues noticed his twisted experiments, they had him fired. To get revenge, Crane became the Scarecrow to try to frighten his enemies to death.

- Crane does not use conventional weaponry. Instead, he invented a Fear Toxin that causes his victims to hallucinate, bringing their worst fears and phobias to life. The gas makes the weak and gangly Crane look like a fearsome predator in the eyes of his prey.

- Even though he preys on the fears of others, the Scarecrow has a fear of his own – bats! Crane has been chiroptophobic (afraid of bats) since his first encounter with the Dark Knight.

- Crane's mastery of fear has come in handy. While locked up in Arkham Asylum, Crane escaped from his cell by scaring two guards into releasing him!

CONFIDENTIAL

BIOGRAPHIES

Matthew K. Manning has written books and comics about Batman, Iron Man, Wolverine, the Legion of Super-Heroes, Spider-Man, the Incredible Hulk, and the Looney Tunes. Most recently, he wrote a history of Batman called *The Batman Vault*.

Erik Doescher is a freelance illustrator and video game designer. He illustrated for a number of comic studios throughout the 1990s, and then moved into video game development and design. However, he has not completely given up on illustrating his favourite comic book characters.

Mike DeCarlo is a contributor of comic art whose range extends from Batman and Iron Man to Bugs Bunny and Scooby-Doo.

Lee Loughridge has been working in comics for more than fifteen years. He currently lives in a tent on the beach.

GLOSSARY

alter ego another side of yourself; a secret identity

anaesthetic drug given to patients by dentists and doctors. Anaesthetic prevents you from feeling pain during a tooth extraction or operation.

chaos total confusion

cowl large, loose hood

device piece of equipment that does a particular job

foe enemy

mentor wise and trusted role model or teacher

sabotaged interfered with a plan, or tried to ruin something

surveyed looked at the whole of a scene or situation

Utility Belt Batman's belt, which holds all of his weaponry and gadgets

DISCUSSION QUESTIONS

1. Do you think Scarecrow is mad? What does it mean to be mad? Discuss your answers.

2. Batman and Batgirl work together to defeat Scarecrow. Do you prefer to work alone or as part of a team? Why?

3. This book has ten illustrations. Which one is your favourite? Why?

WRITING PROMPTS

1. Scarecrow loves to frighten others. What kinds of things scare you? How do you deal with fear? Write about a scary experience.

2. Bruce Wayne's secret identity is Batman. Create your own super hero alter ego. What superpowers do you have? How do you use them to fight crime? Write about it. Then draw a picture of your super hero identity.

3. Write another chapter to this story. What new evil plan does Scarecrow have in mind? How will the Dark Knight fight the villain? You decide.

MORE NEW BATMAN ADVENTURES!

KILLER CROC HUNTER

THE MAKER OF MONSTERS

MAD HATTER'S MOVIE MADNESS

CATWOMAN'S HALLOWEEN HEIST

ROBIN'S FIRST FLIGHT